EGMONT

EGMONT

We bring stories to life

Kiss Chasey
First published in 2006 by E2
an imprint of Hardie Grant Egmont

This edition published 2009
by Egmont Books Limited
239 Kensington High Street
London W8 6SA

Illustrations by Sonia Dixon
Based on original illustration and design by Ash Oswald

ISBN 978 14052 4543 2

1 3 5 7 9 10 8 6 4 2

www.egmont.co.uk

A CIP record for this title is available from the British Library

Printed and bound in the UK

BY
THALIA KALKIPSAKIS

ILLUSTRATIONS BY
SONIA DIXON

BASED ON ORIGINAL ILLUSTRATIONS
BY ASH OSWALD

EGMONT

CHAPTER *ONE

I closed my eyes and puckered up my lips. This was it – my first kiss.

I could hear my best friend Alex next to me. She was talking loudly, telling Callum and me to get ready. Two of Callum's friends were muttering and giggling.

I was breathing through my nose and could smell the pine needles at our feet.

'On your marks,' Alex yelled.

I squeezed my eyes shut even tighter, wondering what my first kiss was going to feel like. Wet? Soft? Slimy and gooey?

I had kissed grown-ups on the cheek before. But I knew that was nothing like this. This was big. This was important. I was going to remember my first kiss for the rest of my life.

'Get set,' Alex said.

She was almost squealing with excitement.

I started breathing faster, too. But I wasn't excited any more. I was scared. I wasn't sure if I wanted to do this with everyone watching.

'Go!' Alex squealed.

I held my breath, puckered my lips again, and waited.

My first kiss!

Nothing happened. I could still hear Callum's friends giggling.

I opened my eyes.

Callum was standing opposite me with one foot in front of the other, like he was about to run a race. He's tall, so he was hunched over to be at my level.

He was leaning forward and frowning as if this was the most important thing in his life.

'Come on, Becky,' Alex said.

She bumped me with her hip. I bumped her straight back. I wasn't sure what else to do. I didn't want to look at Callum.

I have known Callum for years. Our mums are friends, so I see him all the time. But we are linked in other ways, too. Last year we both did speeches at the school concert. And now we're the only kids in our class allowed to use pens instead of pencils.

So, as Alex always says, we're a perfect match.

'Come on!' Alex said again.

'This feels stupid,' Callum said quietly.

His friends started making slurpy kissing noises and wrestling with each other.

I looked down at my feet and kicked at some pine needles. When I looked up again, Callum was looking at me. I think he felt the same as I did – we didn't want to do this with everyone watching.

'Yeah, this is stupid,' I said, turning around to Alex.

But I felt a bit disappointed.

'Becky!' said Alex. She had her hands on her hips, like she always does when she's telling people what to do. 'We've been planning this for days!'

I shrugged. 'Well, it doesn't feel right.'

One of Callum's friends grabbed him around the waist. So Callum dived on top of him. Soon all three of them were rolling in the dusty pine needles, play-fighting and mock-kissing.

Alex looked sternly at me and raised her eyebrows.

'Why don't *you* do it then?' I whispered to Alex.

This whole thing had started because Alex liked Mickey, one of Callum's friends.

But somehow Alex had planned it so that Callum and I had to go first.

Alex shook her head and her cheeks went pink. I giggled. I wasn't used to Alex being shy.

By now the three boys were running among the trees, playing chasey. But they didn't stray far from Alex and me.

Then, as Callum ran past, he tagged me on the arm.

'Becky's it!' he screeched as he ran away, heading for the field.

Of course, I tagged Alex in an instant, and was off after the boys before she could even get her hands off her hips.

It felt good to be running and laughing

again after thinking so much about my first kiss.

But as I caught up with the boys in the middle of the sports field, Alex called out from behind me.

'I've got it!' she yelled.

We all stopped running and looked at her. As she reached us, she did a dramatic leap and spread her arms out for effect.

'Kiss chasey!' Alex said, as she landed.

Mickey nodded and smiled.

But Callum laughed. 'Yeah, but you girls can't catch us boys!' he said.

By now I had my hands on *my* hips. 'We can catch you, no problem!' I said.

We all started giggling then, and trying

to work out the rules of kiss chasey.

I smiled over at Callum and he smiled back.

We still had a chance at our first kiss.

CHAPTER TWO

At lunchtime the next day, we all ran laughing to the pine tree area, ready to play kiss chasey.

None of us really knew how to play. We couldn't work out how to tag some-one with a kiss. How do you kiss when you're running?

So we all decided that if you were tagged like normal, you had to stop running and let the other person kiss you.

As I put my foot in the circle, I looked over at Callum. He was frowning a bit, with his hands on his knees. But his eyes were shining.

I like it when his eyes look like that.

Alex bent down and started counting out our feet. 'Eeney meeney miney mo, catch a tadpole by its toe . . .'

I had an image in my mind of Callum chasing me to a quiet spot, maybe at the back of the pine tree area.

When we were by ourselves, I would slow down. He would tag me when no-one else was looking. And then . . .

I never imagined what I would do if

I was it. So when all the counting finished and I was left with my foot in the circle, I just stood there, surprised.

I was it!

I could see Alex among the trees, running towards the pitch. But as I turned around, I realised I had no idea where Callum was. I hadn't even seen him run off.

I started dashing between the pine trees, jumping over tree roots and checking behind the trunks. But I couldn't find Callum. In fact, I couldn't find any of my friends.

My heart was pumping fast. I ran out of the shade of the pine trees and looked across the field.

There, standing in a group on the cricket pitch, were Callum and his friends.

For a moment I wasn't sure what to do. *Does Callum want me to run down and tag him on the pitch, with everyone watching? Why is he just standing there with his friends?*

But then Callum's words from yesterday came back to me. He didn't think I could catch him. That was why he was just standing on the grass!

In an instant, I started sprinting towards the pitch. I could feel my fists clenched tight and hear the gravel crunching and sliding under my feet.

I had to catch Callum.

He was tall and good at sport. But still

I had to catch him. I had to prove him
wrong.

I was over the fence and speeding
across the grass before Callum even
noticed I was coming. He jolted when he
did see me. Then he turned around and
started sprinting away.

As I dashed past his friends, they laughed and Mickey yelled out, 'Go get him, Becky!'

But I didn't even look at them. All I could think of was moving my legs and pumping my arms.

All I could think of was catching Callum.

When he thought he was a safe distance away, Callum turned around and called out, 'Catch me if you can!'

Then he laughed and ran backwards for a while, as if he didn't have to try very hard.

But I just kept on running, like a train with no breaks. I didn't even waste breath on answering him or laughing.

I was going to catch that boy . . .

CHAPTER THREE

I stayed focused and kept running.

Callum was still laughing and running backwards, but he wasn't moving very fast like that. The distance between us was getting smaller.

Callum must have noticed I was getting closer, because suddenly he stopped smiling. He turned around and bolted.

But the time he had wasted calling out

and running backwards meant that I was close. Now I was right on his heels.

I kept pumping my arms and breathing in rhythm. He was fast, but I was close enough now. I just had to stay with him.

If he slowed down to jump the fence or even change direction, that's when I would have him. I was right behind him, thinking about reaching out and tagging him.

Then suddenly, Callum fell.

I was so close behind him that I had to jump over him to avoid falling on him.

I looked down as I jumped, and saw his tall body in a strange tangle beneath me.

Then, as I landed, Callum let out a sobbing cry that seemed to echo around the pitch and back. It was the kind of cry that kids our age normally only let out in front of their parents – groaning and desperate and really scared.

Something was very, very wrong.

Panting, I found my balance and looked down at Callum.

'Are you OK?' I asked, even though it was clear that he wasn't.

Callum was crying really loudly. His friends ran up to us.

'What did you do?' Mickey yelled at me.

I just looked at him, stunned and scared about what was happening. But I didn't answer, it seemed like a strange question.

'He needs help!' I screamed at them.

Then I turned around and bolted for the staffroom.

After that our teacher, Mrs Tran, came over and helped Callum up. They walked slowly to the sick bay with a bunch of kids crowded around them.

I felt sick from the running and the worry. Alex was holding my hand and asking what had happened. But I couldn't talk yet. I kept hearing Callum's cry echoing in my head.

I had never heard a boy make a sound like that before.

What had happened to him?

Callum disappeared into the sick bay with the teacher and his friends.

Oh no!
What happened
to Callum?

Everyone else ran off to play.

Alex and I stood outside the old door that's closest to the sick bay.

'What happened?' Alex asked for the millionth time.

Her eyes looked big and scared.

I shook my head. 'I don't know,' I said. 'He just fell . . .'

For a moment we just looked at each other. Then I pushed at the door and walked inside.

It was strange seeing the corridor so empty. Usually it's full of kids and bags and noise. Now it seemed like a place I'd never been before.

Alex was clutching my sleeve, like we

were in a horror movie or something.

We tiptoed past a couple of doors to reach the sick bay. Lucky for us, the staff-room was further down the hall.

Alex and I held hands and listened at the sick bay door.

'I've called your parents,' we heard Mrs Tran say. 'We'll meet them at the hospital. I'm going to bring my car around to the front of the school. OK?'

I didn't hear Callum reply, but then the door opened and Mrs Tran rushed out. She didn't even see Alex and me. Or if she did, she was thinking about other things.

For a while I listened at the door, but I couldn't hear anything. It didn't seem like Callum's friends were with him. Maybe they had already been sent outside.

Alex tugged at my hand like she wanted to go outside, too.

But I had to see Callum. I let go of Alex's hand, pushed at the door and went into the sick bay.

CHAPTER FOUR

Inside, Callum was alone on the bed. He had ice packs on his shoulder, and wet cheeks.

He lay still, as if it hurt to move.

I tried to smile, but I didn't know what to say. A flood of questions filled my mind. *What happened? Are you OK? Do you know what's wrong?* But none of them seemed the right thing to say.

In the end, it was Callum who spoke first. I wasn't expecting him to talk, but when he did, my throat went tight.

Without moving his head, Callum said quietly, 'Becky, why did you trip me up?'

'I – I didn't trip you up!' I said.

Then I heard the door behind me, and Mrs Tran came in.

'Outside please, Becky,' she said quickly.

So I had to go outside with Alex while Mrs Tran took Callum to hospital.

When Callum's mum Debbie is happy she gets funny laugh lines around her eyes. I like it when she looks like that. But that was the last kind of face I was expecting to see when mum and I knocked on the door that night.

But Debbie was smiling, and she kept smiling when she looked at me, which was even more of a surprise.

My mum and Debbie had already spoken on the phone, so we knew what had happened at the hospital.

Callum had a broken collarbone. That meant he had to wear a sling for six whole weeks. It was the arm that he writes with, so he was going to have trouble writing, too. And as for basketball . . .

It was pretty bad, really. So I had no

idea why Debbie looked like she had been laughing.

'Come in, ladies,' Debbie said.

Mum gave her a bunch of flowers and they went into the kitchen to find a vase.

Normally I would have run off to find Callum, but I wasn't sure if he wanted to see me.

Plus, I didn't know what he'd said to Debbie. *Was he still saying that I tripped him? Did he tell her we'd been playing kiss chasey?*

'He's in the extension, Becky,' Debbie called out.

She still had those laugh lines around her eyes.

I started walking slowly up the hall.

Before I had gone far, I heard Debbie whisper something to mum.

Then my mum let out a shriek and said, 'Aren't they a little young for that?'

Then they both started laughing.

I heard Debbie say, 'Our little babies are growing up!'

At least now I knew why Debbie had been laughing. Callum had told her about kiss chasey!

Now I picked up my pace, frowning as I walked. I couldn't understand why Callum had told his mum about kiss chasey. *Why would he do that?*

So when I got to the extension, I wasn't exactly in a happy mood.

Callum was lying on the couch, trying to play his Game Boy with one hand.

I slumped down in a chair just as I heard his game finish.

Callum threw the Game Boy on to the

floor. I don't think he could play with one hand. For a while we just sat there, saying nothing.

Then I leaned forward in the chair. 'Why did you tell your mum about kiss chasey?' I asked.

'Because I broke my collarbone,' he said, without looking at me. 'Or didn't you notice?'

'Look, I'm really sorry about that,' I said.

But I was getting annoyed. I picked up the Game Boy.

'So you're sorry you tripped me up?' Callum said, moving to look at me. I could tell it hurt to move.

Why did he keep saying that?

'No,' I said. 'I didn't trip you, Cal.'

'Not on purpose,' said Callum.

He was in a pretty bad mood, and I told him so.

After that, Callum stopped talking to me. He just lay on the couch, frowning into space.

I sat in the chair, playing his Game Boy. I felt sorry for Callum – a broken collarbone was pretty bad. But I felt angry with him, too.

Why did he keep saying that I tripped him up?

When it was time to go home. I didn't even say bye to Callum. I just ran out to mum, feeling cross.

I was almost glad that I hadn't caught
Callum when we played kiss chasey.

CHAPTER FIVE

The next morning at school, Callum wasn't there. But other than that, nothing seemed unusual. At least, that was how the day started.

During assembly, I was up the front in the recorder group, playing the national anthem. We're pretty good these days – nice and loud.

At the start of the year, the headmaster

used to set up the microphone in front of us, but now he doesn't even bother.

We ended with a really loud note that seemed to echo through the school.

But that was when everything stopped being normal.

Instead of talking about the latest excursion to the zoo, or how much rubbish was lying around, the headmaster started talking about something else.

Along with British bulldogs, where you get tackled to the ground, kiss chasey was now officially banned from our school.

Of course, that was fine with me. Callum was being so mean, I didn't care about kiss chasey any more. Well, not really.

But as the headmaster kept talking, I star-ted to realise that the rest of the school wasn't looking at him.

Being up the front for recorder meant that I could see everyone's faces. And they were all looking at me.

The younger kids had that dumb, blank look they get. But they were definitely looking past the headmaster, at me.

Even the teachers were looking at me. Most of them had that 'teacher frown' that they do so well. But Mrs Tran was smiling, just like Debbie last night.

News gets around pretty fast in my school!

Even the kids in my class were giggling

or whispering and looking at me. Some of the boys were scowling like they hated me.

In fact, the only people who *weren't* looking at me were Alex and Mickey. They were looking at each other, and talking quietly. I couldn't hear what they were saying, but Alex definitely didn't look happy.

I wasn't happy either.

Callum's collarbone wasn't my fault!

But everyone was blaming me.

When he finally got to the end of his lecture, the headmaster said, 'I'm sure we won't have any more trouble with kiss chasey now, will we?'

Then, in front of the whole school, he turned and looked at me.

Lunchtime was pretty bad too. I was sitting on the steps with Alex when a bunch of little kids ran up, giggling and whispering.

'That's her there!' one of them shouted, pointing at me.

Then they all ran away, like I was

going to eat them up.

Alex laughed. 'You're famous now, Becky!'

But I wasn't laughing.

Then Mickey and Brad walked up, and things got serious.

'You're lucky we don't bash you up,' Brad said to me.

'It was an accident, you idiot,' Alex yelled. She stood up and put her hands on her hips.

I started to think about where I would run if I needed to get away quickly. But I didn't think he really meant it.

'Well, there are accidents,' Mickey said, all serious. 'And there are *accidents*.'

'What does that mean?' I asked.

But the boys just gave me an angry look and walked away.

'Geez!' I said, shaking my head.

This was getting silly.

'Ooooh, I *hate* Mickey,' Alex said. Her mouth was tight. 'He's so . . . yuk.'

'You didn't think that yesterday,' I said, and raised my eyebrows.

'Yeah, well,' Alex said, as she sat down and picked up her sandwich. 'That was before.'

After that we just sat there eating quietly. But I was thinking it all through. Alex didn't seem to like Mickey any more.

How do you know if the person you like is

worth it? And how can you tell if he likes you?

I used to feel sure that Callum liked me – the way he used to steal my bag or my pen, like he wanted me to notice him. Or he would pull my hair like he wanted to be near me.

He just always seemed to be around.

But maybe I was wrong. Maybe Callum didn't like me like that.

When I started thinking about our game of kiss chasey yesterday, I started to think I had made a mistake.

The way Callum had stood on the pitch, and how hard he had tried to get away – maybe Callum had never wanted to kiss me after all.

CHAPTER SIX

Over the weekend I didn't see Callum or Alex. But by Monday morning, I was feel-ing better. News travels fast at my school. But it turns into old news pretty quickly, too.

When I got to school, Alex wasn't there yet.

I did a slow walk around – that kind of walk where you check things out, but pretend you're totally relaxed. Secretly, I wanted to see if Callum was back at school yet.

Once Callum came back, I wanted things to go back to normal – just us goofing around, like we always did.

I didn't like Callum or his friends being angry with me. I just wanted our game of kiss chasey to disappear like a bad dream.

As I passed a group of little kids, they all stopped talking and looked at me. But they stayed quiet.

I pretended not to notice. But as I walked around the corner, I half-looked back at them, trying to hear if they were going to say anything.

Big mistake.

'Hey! Watch where you're going!'

Mickey was standing right there. Five centimetres from my face. I was so close I could have kissed him. I had been so busy looking back at the little kids that I hadn't seen where I was going.

Mickey jumped back and brushed himself off like I had fleas.

'Oh, sorry,' I mumbled.

But I wasn't looking at Mickey.

Callum was sitting on his bag with his arm in a bright blue sling.

I just stood there, looking at him. His eyes looked nice against his sling. But things had gotten off to a bad start.

'So,' I said, trying to sound like I was cool, but I felt weird. 'How's your arm?' I asked Callum.

'My arm's fine,' Callum said. 'But my collarbone hurts like anything.'

His friends laughed.

My cheeks started to burn. Now I had no idea what to do. Callum was looking at me like he was waiting for me to go away.

So that's what I did.

I walked off, feeling really bad. Now I was sure that I had got it all wrong. Callum didn't like me. At least, not in a kissing kind of way.

But that didn't matter now. It didn't even seem like we were friends any more. Somehow, playing kiss chasey had wrecked everything.

Alex didn't make it to school until when the bell went. That's pretty normal for Alex.

So, of course, there was heaps to talk

about as we sat down for class. I couldn't start the day without first talking to Alex. Not when there was the weekend and boys to discuss.

I was right in the middle of telling Alex about what Callum had said that morning, when I heard a strange voice yelling:

'Everyone listening, please!'

I stopped talking to Alex and sat up straight.

There, standing in front of our class, was an emergency teacher. She was really tall and had a big jaw like a man.

But that wasn't the worst of it.

The worst part was what she was saying. 'I'll be teaching you for the next few weeks,' she said in a booming voice.

Few weeks! Suddenly, Callum and kiss chasey weren't my only problems. Mrs Tran was my favourite teacher ever.

The emergency teacher kept talking about all the work she was going to give us. But I couldn't concentrate.

What was wrong with Mrs Tran? It wasn't like her to leave us with a mean teacher. Was she sick? Had the boys finally given her a nervous breakdown?

I had to know what was going on.

'What's wrong with Mrs Tran?' I called out.

The emergency teacher frowned. She looked even meaner when she did that. 'No calling out in class,' she said.

Straight away, I put up my hand. We were allowed to ask questions, weren't we?

But the emergency teacher frowned even more. 'You're Rebecca Olsen, aren't you?' she said.

I nodded, feeling worried.

Normally I wouldn't mind if a new teacher knew my name. You never know what people have been saying.

It could be something really good like, *There's Becky Olsen. She's going to be a famous artist one day.*

Or maybe, *There's Becky Olsen. She's the kindest, smartest, prettiest girl in the school.*

Well, a girl can only dream!

But after the events of the past few days, I had a feeling that it would be more like, *There's Becky Olsen. She broke a boy's collarbone playing kiss chasey. And what's worse — he doesn't even like her like that!*

In the end the emergency teacher didn't answer my question. She just kept talking about how she was going to 'do things' and what she 'expected from us'.

So now I was stuck in a class with a bunch of boys *and* a teacher who hated me. And all because of playing kiss chasey.

CHAPTER
SEVEN

'Yay! Thanks, Mum!'

Alex and I ran, cheering and clapping down the hall into my room.

'That's five *altogether*,' mum called out after us.

'Thanks, Mum!' I called out again, before I shut my bedroom door.

Finally, something good was happening to me. Mum was letting me have my birthday party at the movies. But even better, we were allowed to watch the movie without any adults.

'So, who are you going to invite?' Alex asked.

She was already sitting at my desk with a piece of paper in front of her. She wrote our names at the top of the list.

I lay down on my bed. 'Only three more, hey?'

We were both quiet, thinking.

Three weeks ago, it would have been easy. Alex and me, plus Callum and his friends Mickey and Brad. That made five.

Perfect!

I liked the idea of inviting boys to my

party. And three weeks ago, Callum and his friends were part of our group. But we didn't hang around with them any more. Mickey was still acting like he hated us. And I wasn't talking much to Callum.

'What about Darcy and her friends?' Alex asked.

'Yeah, Darcy's cool,' I said.

But I was thinking about Callum.

'Only, there's four in her group,' Alex said, scribbling out some names. 'That's too many.'

We were quiet for a while. I thought about how things used to be, before we played kiss chasey. Before the mean emergency teacher arrived.

Alex started drawing flower patterns on the paper.

'What do you think is wrong with Mrs Tran?' I asked. 'She must be pretty sick to be away for this long.'

'Dunno,' Alex said, still drawing. 'Hey, what about the Basketball Girls?'

'Yeah, I like them,' I said.

We all call Angie and Claire the Basketball Girls because they always play basketball at lunchtime.

'Except that's only four for the party,' Alex said.

'That's OK,' I said. 'We'll still have fun.'

But I didn't feel as excited any more. My birthday list didn't feel quite right.

After Alex went home, I kept thinking about Mrs Tran, and Callum.

I used to look forward to going to school. Mrs Tran is a great teacher. And Callum is my second-best friend.

At least he *used* to be.

I pulled out a fresh piece of paper and started drawing a border around the edge. It took ages. There were a lot of tiny leaves and flowers to colour in. When I'd finished the paper had a tangled green vine with red and yellow flowers all around the edge.

It looked pretty good.

I stared at the blank part in the middle of the paper.

If I wrote a letter to Callum, I wondered, *would he forgive me? Would he be my friend again?*

But I didn't really think anything could make Callum be my friend again.

I added a few more leaves to the border.

Then I started writing in the middle.
Slowly. Carefully. In my very best writing:

Dear Mrs Tran,
GET WELL SOON!
We miss you.

I did hearts instead of dots. And, inside
the two 'Os' for 'soon' I did two sad faces.

Then I turned the paper over and wrote
'Becky Olsen' on the back.

Maybe I couldn't fix things with Callum. But I could write a note to Mrs Tran.

Even if that doesn't seem like much, it felt good to be doing something.

CHAPTER EIGHT

The next day, class started out as usual —
with the emergency teacher yelling,
'Rebecca, quiet please!'

Actually, now that I think about it,
class usually started with the emergency
teacher yelling *at me*.

Sometimes it was because I was talking.

And last week I spoke back to her about
my pen licence.

Now that Callum could hardly write, I was the only one in our class allowed to write with a pen. I had worked really hard to earn that pen licence with Mrs Tran.

But the emergency teacher had said that she didn't do things like that. She said that I would have to use a grey lead until *everyone* in the class was ready to move on to pens.

I'll never be able to use a pen, then!

Judging from the messy boys' writing, that would mean waiting until high school!

But today was definitely one morning when I didn't want the emergency teacher yelling at me.

I had been quietly handing around my card for Mrs Tran so that everyone could sign it.

Then Darcy had asked me, 'What if we don't miss Mrs Tran? Do we still have to sign our name?'

I just shrugged.

When I got back to my desk, I whispered to Alex, 'I'm glad we crossed Darcy off the party list.'

That was when the trouble started.

Darcy was waving the card around like it was a flag.

'Darcy, are you passing around notes?' asked the teacher.

'No, Miss,' said Darcy, in a sickly sweet voice. It made me wonder why I ever thought of inviting Darcy to my party.

'Give that to me, please.'

And before my eyes, the exact thing happened that I definitely didn't want to happen. Darcy passed my card up to the teacher.

We were all quiet while she read it. I could see her looking at my writing — I had done it in pen. Then she turned it over and read all the names.

'Who did this?' she asked.

But the strange thing was, she wasn't angry. She had a sad sort of look on her face.

I put up my hand.

'Very good work, Rebecca,' she said.

Then she pulled a big envelope from her desk drawer and put the card inside.

'A few more people need to sign their name,' she said, as she put the envelope on my desk. 'Once everyone's done that, I'll make sure Mrs Tran gets the card.'

Then the emergency teacher smiled at me. And for a split second, she even stopped looking mean.

By late morning, I had everyone's name on the card, except one. It didn't matter how many times I sent the card around the room, it always came back without Callum's name on it.

I knew Callum could hardly write with his left hand. But that didn't matter. I wanted everyone to sign the card – that was the whole point.

When the bell rang for lunch, I slipped over to Callum's desk. He was a bit slow packing away his work with one hand.

Soon it was just us left in the classroom.

'Lucky last!' I said, and put the card on Callum's desk.

But Callum shook his head. 'Have you seen how messy my writing is now?' he said.

'That doesn't matter!' I said. 'Mrs Tran won't mind.'

He shook his head again. His shoulder still looked stiff.

'Go on,' I said gently.

I handed him a pen and held the card down so it wouldn't move around.

Don't worry about your handwriting!

Callum sighed. But, slowly, he started to write his name.

It was quiet in the room. I could hear Callum breathing as he worked.

'Not bad!' I said, when he had finished.

'Not bad for a prep kid!' Callum said, and laughed.

I laughed too.

'It's your birthday soon, isn't it?' said Callum.

I nodded, putting the card back in its envelope. But I could hear my heart beating now.

'Doing anything good?' he asked.

'Um, maybe the movies,' I mumbled.

But my mind was racing. Callum had been to all of my birthday parties so far. *Should I invite him to this one after all?*

'Sounds good!' he said, as he walked out to lunch.

I was left alone in the classroom, wondering what was going on.

Was Callum still my friend or not?

CHAPTER nine

'I'll give it to him,' said Alex, her eyes sparkling just like the day Callum and I were meant to kiss.

I shook my head and held on tight to the invitation in my hand.

'But he'd be the only boy,' I said.

Alex shrugged. 'That doesn't matter.'

It was lunchtime, and only two days before my birthday party.

The invitation wasn't for Alex or the Basketball Girls — they had already said they could come.

In my hand was a birthday invitation for Callum. Inside, around all the details about the party, I had written,

Birthday Party

Dear Callum,
I'm sorry about your collarbone.
If you're still angry, that's OK.
You don't have to come.

But now I felt nervous about giving it to him. I didn't even know if Callum was my friend any more.

'Come on, Becky,' Alex said, her hands on her hips. 'Just give it to him.'

'No,' I said. I thought about how angry Callum had been. 'He won't want to come anyway.'

I started to put the invitation in my pocket. But Alex snatched it away from me.

'Well, if you won't give it to him, I will,' she said.

She started to walk away with the invitation. At first I didn't know what to do. I just stood there with my mouth open.

But then I started to feel angry.

This was *my* party. And Callum used to be *my* friend.

This had nothing to do with Alex. *Maybe if she hadn't started talking about kissing in the first place, then Callum and I would still be friends. Why did I always let Alex take over?*

I felt anger surging through me, and started to run.

I caught up with Alex in a flash and

snatched the invitation back before she knew what was happening.

'It's my party, Alex!' I yelled.

Alex stopped and stared at me.

Straight away I felt bad for yelling. 'Callum's *my* friend,' I said quietly.

'Oh,' Alex said, and looked at her feet.

'I'll give it to him myself,' I said, and tried to smile.

'OK,' Alex said.

But I kept standing there, feeling bad.

Then Alex started to smile. 'Well, hurry up then!' she said. 'I'll meet you at the steps.'

Alex winked and then headed the other way. That's one of my favourite things about Alex – she doesn't hold a grudge.

I gulped and started looking around for Callum. Now I *had* to give him the invitation.

'Becky, wait!' Callum said, running after me.

I had just given him the invitation, but I didn't hang around to watch him open it.

'I'm not angry,' Callum said, when he had caught up with me.

'That's good,' I said, quietly, looking at Callum's shoes. His feet are really big these days.

'Yeah, I realised that you didn't trip me,'

Callum said, smiling.

'Really?'

Now I forgot to feel shy. This was something new.

'If you tripped me up, that would mean you caught me,' Callum said, laughing. 'And there's no way you did that!'

'Oh really?' I said, looking up at him.

But I was laughing too. Now it didn't seem to matter what had really happened.

After that, we talked properly for the first time since we played kiss chasey. Not about anything big, but it still felt great.

'So, are we still friends?' I said after a while.

'Sure,' Callum said, his eyes shining.

We're still friends!

He tucked the invitation into his sling and held out his left hand for me to shake.

For a moment, I wasn't sure what to do. It's not like I go around shaking people's hands every day.

Then I slipped my hand into his and we shook.

I wasn't looking at Callum's face, but his hand felt nice and strong in my hand.

'Friends,' Callum said, and walked away.

I headed for Alex and the steps.

I couldn't stop grinning. It felt great to be friends with Callum again. And there was something about that handshake that made me feel brilliant.

CHAPTER TEN

I couldn't help feeling sorry for poor Callum. He must have really missed playing basketball because of his collarbone.

I had been worried that he wouldn't have anyone to talk to at my movie party – him being the only boy.

But as it turned out, Callum did more talking than anyone.

He kept asking Angie and Claire about

their basketball team, and whether their coach was any good.

The three of them stood, huddled together in the cinema foyer, talking about dribbling and drills and shots at the basket.

They kept moving their bodies like they were really playing and taking shots in the air with pretend balls.

Callum looked like he was itching to really play.

After a while, Alex raised her eyebrows and looked at me as if to say, *What's going on here?*

I just shrugged. I was pleased Callum was getting on well with the Basketball Girls, but I started to wonder whether

Callum really liked Angie or Claire. I mean, in a kissing kind of way.

Maybe that was why he hadn't wanted to kiss me, I suddenly thought. *Because he really liked one of them!*

Maybe he really likes Angie or Claire!

So I just stood there, at my own party, wondering how I would feel if Callum kissed someone else.

It wasn't exactly my favourite part of

the day. But then I decided that I really didn't mind. I had nearly lost Callum as a friend because of kiss chasey. All that kissing stuff had been a lot more trouble than it was worth.

If Callum wanted to kiss someone else, then that was fine with me. Just as long as he was still my friend, I didn't care what he did.

After a while, Callum looked over at me and said, 'Becky, you should play basketball.'

I shook my head, but I was smiling. 'I'm too short,' I said.

Callum grinned. 'You're fast enough, though!' he said.

We all laughed.

By the time we went in for the movie, I was feeling good. I had all my favourite friends with me on my birthday. No more problems because of kiss chasey, and no adults around.

What more could a girl ask for?

Everyone else was having fun too.

Alex started telling rude jokes to Angie and Claire.

They were all laughing really loud as they sat down together. So it turned out that they sat next to each, then me, then Callum on the end.

'Do you want to sit next to someone else?' I asked Callum. If he liked Angie or Claire, then he wouldn't want to be stuck with me.

'You're the birthday girl, aren't you?' Callum said.

Then the lights dimmed and the ads started on the screen.

'Besides,' he said softly, 'you're the first girl I've held hands with.'

I looked at him in the dark. I wasn't sure if I had heard him right.

'What do you mean?' I asked.

I had to lean in so he could hear me above the noise of the ads.

'When we shook hands the other day at school,' came back Callum's voice in the dark. 'That's almost the same as holding hands.'

Then, in the dim light, I could see Callum holding out his good hand. It was palm up, like he wanted to hold my hand.

By now, my heart was pounding even louder than the noise from the screen.

At least, that was how it felt.

I glanced over at Alex and the others. But they were laughing about one of the ads. They still weren't doing a very good job of keeping quiet.

Slowly, I reached out and slipped my hand into Callum's. We rested our hands on the seat rest between us.

His hand felt warm, like he was holding me in a hug. It felt wonderful.

A couple of times during the movie, Alex shook her bag of sweets at Callum and me. But she didn't realise that we were holding hands.

Holding hands in the dark like that felt like the biggest, best secret.

When the movie finished, we stopped holding hands, but we still seemed joined somehow.

As we walked out into the foyer, Callum smiled at me and I smiled back.

'Why are you smiling?' asked Alex.

I just shrugged. 'I'm happy!' I said.

I wasn't going to tell Alex what had happened. Not for a while at least – it had nothing to do with her.

It was something special and secret, between Callum and me.

This time we didn't have Alex counting us down for a kiss, or the adults laughing, or the whole school whispering about us. This was none of their business.

Callum is the first boy I ever held hands with. I'm going to remember how that feels for the rest of my life.

THE END

**If you loved this GO GIRL!
story, why not look for the
others in the series, available
in all good bookshops.**

**For more information,
go to our website at
www.egmont.co.uk**

meet THE Go GIRL! GIRLS and JOIN THE FUN.

REAL LIFE, REAL GIRLS
Go GIRL!